Library of Congress Cataloging in Publication Data

Keats, Ezra Jack.　　Dreams.　　I. Title.
PZ7.K2253Dr　　[E]　　73–15857
ISBN 0–02–749610–4

EZRA JACK KEATS

MACMILLAN PUBLISHING CO., INC.
NEW YORK

For Mitsue Ishitake,
Sachiko Saionji,
Yosuke Seki,
and my friends
of the Ohanashi Caravan

It was hot.
After supper Roberto came
to his window to talk with Amy.
"Look what I made in school today—
a paper mouse!"
"Does it do anything?" Amy asked.
Roberto thought for a while.
"I don't know," he said. Then he put
the mouse on the window sill.

As it grew darker, the city got quieter.
"Bedtime, Roberto," called his mother.
"Bedtime for you, too,"
other mothers called.
"Good-night, Amy."
"Good-night, Roberto."
"G-o-o-o-o-d-night!" echoed the parrot.
Soon they were all in bed.

Someone began to dream.

Soon everybody was dreaming—
except one person.

Somehow Roberto just couldn't fall asleep.
It got later and later.

Finally he got up
and went to the window.
What he saw down in the street
made him gasp!

There was Archie's cat!
A big dog had chased him into a box.
The dog snarled.
"He's trapped!" thought Roberto.
"What should I do?"

Then it happened!
His pajama sleeve
brushed the paper mouse
off the window sill.
It sailed away from him.

Down it fell,
turning this way
and that,
casting a big shadow
on the wall.

The shadow grew bigger—
and bigger—

and BIGGER!
The dog howled and ran away.

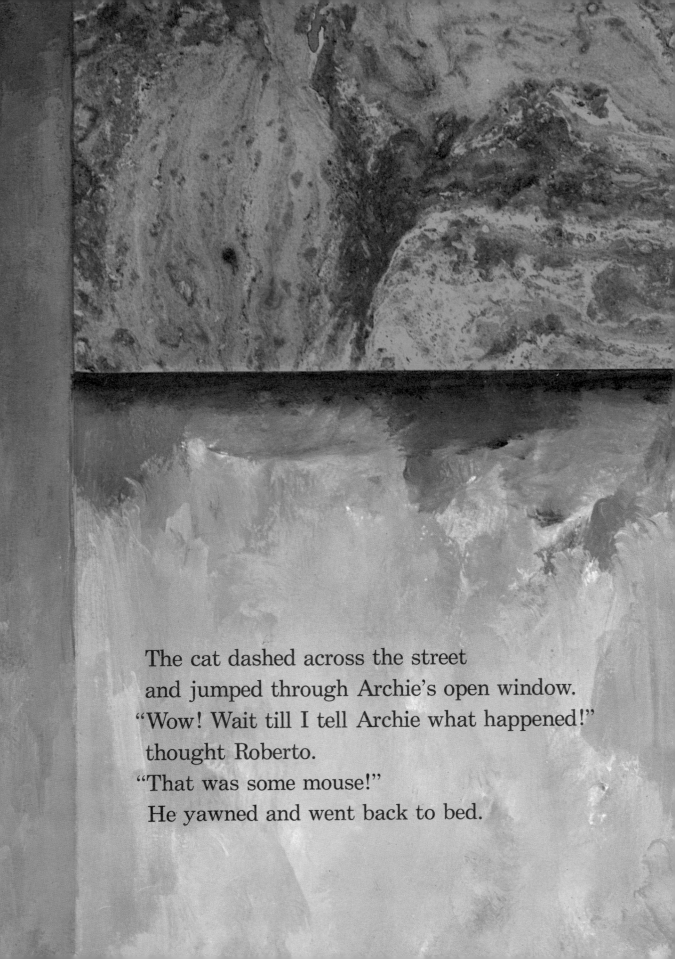

The cat dashed across the street
and jumped through Archie's open window.
"Wow! Wait till I tell Archie what happened!"
thought Roberto.
"That was some mouse!"
He yawned and went back to bed.

Morning came, and everybody
was getting up.
Except one person.

Roberto was fast asleep,
dreaming.

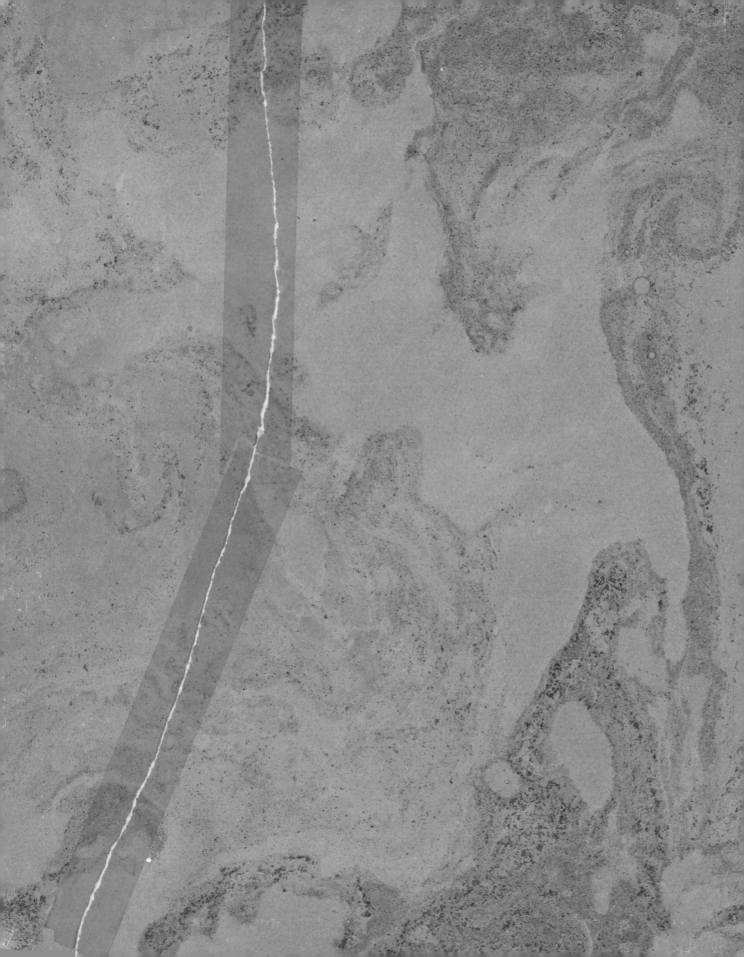